The Boy Who Feared the Wind

Written and Illustrated by

Annia Faith

Reader acclaim for ...
THE BOY WHO FEARED THE WIND

❝In *The Boy Who Feared the Wind*, Annia Faith has woven a relevant tale of a boy who overcomes his fear, discovers courage, and takes ownership of his emotions in a way that allows him to thrive. The author's engaging writing is paired with artful illustrations to create a children's book that is powerful in its simplicity and relevant in its message.

Kayla Gahagan
Author
Rapid City, SD

❝Most notable tales are genuine and straightforward as is this story. It has a simple message with a unique blend of engaging dialogue and creative illustrations. It is a story that has the Icarian touch with a happy ending. *The Boy Who Feared The Wind* will be a delight to young readers of all ages for years to come.

Mark A. Clarke
Author
Ghent, NY

❝Instantly became a favorite story of mine! It found a place in my heart and will soon find a place on my bookshelf! Brought me back to when I was a child myself and scared of so many things. The author is relatable, and I cherish the story.

Megan Cotter
Homemaker
Rapid City, SD

More acclaim on page 38

THE BOY WHO FEARED THE WIND

WRITTEN AND ILLUSTRATED BY

ANNIA FAITH

CCE PUBLISHING
EDGEWATER, FLORIDA

Published by
CCE PUBLISHING
ccepublishing.com
Edgewater, Florida

Printed in the United Sates of America

ISBN 979-8-9892843-0-6

To my little brother, Taiden,
who once feared the wind.

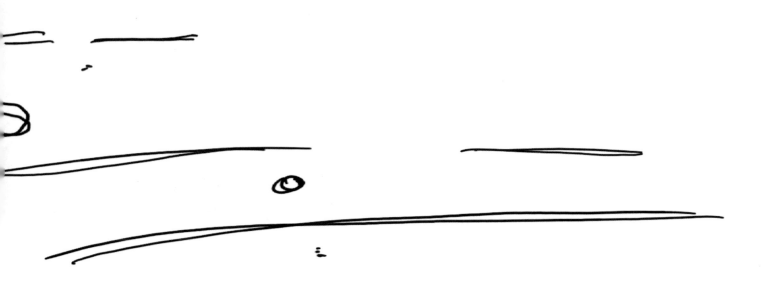

ONCE THERE WAS A BOY WHO FEARED THE WIND
BECAUSE IT PICKED HIM UP AND
TRIED TO CARRY HIM AWAY.

THE BOY RESISTED WITH A FIGHT.
SO THE WIND LET HIM GO,
AND HE CAME CRASHING DOWN.

THE KINDHEARTED WIND APOLOGIZED,
BUT THE BOY ZIPPED AWAY.

He didn't go outside for days,
unwilling to let the wind see his face.
The wind was feeling bad and tried
everything to get the boy to come out again.

THE WIND SENT BALLOONS AND KITES,

EVEN BUBBLES THAT POPPED IN THE SUNLIGHT.

THE WIND SENT BIRDS TO THE PORCH TO PLAY,

BUT THE BOY TURNED AWAY,

HIS HEART HIDDEN IN THE SHADOWS OF DISMAY.

"LEAVE ME ALONE!" THE BOY CRIED.
THE WIND LOOKED DOWN AND SIGHED.

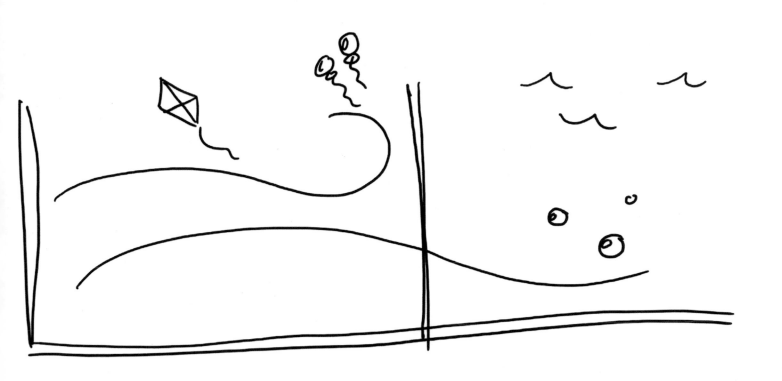

"IF THAT IS WHAT YOU WISH.
I ONLY HOPE FOR YOU TO REACH GREAT HEIGHTS,
BUT I GUESS I'LL LEAVE
SO YOU'RE NOT BEDRIDDEN FROM FRIGHT."

So, THE WIND LEFT,

AND THE VERY NEXT DAY,

THE BOY CAME OUT.

He breathed in, breathed out,

felt relieved beyond doubt.

But something was missing.

THE LEAVES WEREN'T RUSTLING,

THERE WAS NO FRESHNESS IN THE AIR,

AND NO BREEZE CAME ABOUT BLOWING HIS HAIR.

THE BOY THOUGHT OF THE WIND
AND THE FIRST DAY THEY MET.
SURE, HE WAS AFRAID,
BUT THERE WAS A THRILL LIKE NO OTHER
THAT BURNED INSIDE HIM LIKE A BLAZE.

THE BOY WANTED THAT FEELING AGAIN,
SO HE CRIED OUT TO THE WIND.
"OH, PLEASE COME BACK!
I'M SORRY I RAN AWAY FROM YOU.
I WON'T BE AFRAID ANY LONGER."

THE WIND RUSHED THROUGH WITH A GUST OF DELIGHT,
AND THE BOY CLOSED HIS EYES, FEARING FOR HIS LIFE.

"I KNEW YOU'D REMEMBER," THE WIND REPLIED.
"IT'S OKAY TO BE SCARED.
JUST DON'T LET FEAR RULE YOUR LIFE."

THE BOY NODDED AND SAID,
"OKAY, I'M READY TO GO."
HE TRUSTED THE WIND WITH ALL HIS SOUL.

THE WIND SMILED AND SWIRLED,
AND PICKED THE BOY OFF HIS FEET.

AND HE LAUGHED WITH SUCH JOY
THAT SOUNDED INCREDIBLY SWEET.

THE BOY REACHED INTO THE AIR,
ALMOST TOUCHING THE SKY,
AND THE THRILL CAME BACK,
MAKING HIM FEEL ALIVE.

WHEN THE WIND LIFTED HIM HIGH,

HE FELT SO FREE,

NO LONGER HELD DOWN

BY THE WEIGHT OF GRAVITY.

SO EVEN THOUGH THIS BOY
ONCE FEARED THE WIND,
HE LET THE WIND CARRY HIM
AND HIS FEARS FLEW AWAY.

Acknowledgements

I am filled with immense gratitude for the support and encouragement I received throughout this journey of writing and creating "The Boy Who Feared the Wind." Without help, this book would not have been possible:

First, Taiden, my sweet little brother, who was once this boy. You have grown so much, and I am so proud of the overcomer you've become. Without you, this story wouldn't exist, and I'm so glad it does.

To my parents, who have created an environment for my passion and creativity to thrive as I've grown. Thank you for helping me become the young woman that I am today. I will be forever grateful.

To my extended family, and your constant support.

To Pam, who provided opportunities and connected me with people who made this entire process possible. Without you, I would not be where I am today. Thank you for growing me into a diligent and admirable young woman who doesn't forget the people who got her to where she is.

To Kate, Jessie and Mark, who guided and mentored me throughout my journey as an aspiring author. To my wonderful agent, Cindy, who helped me bring this book to life.

To my dear friends, for their endless encouragement and excitement that help me stay confident.

Lastly, a special thank you to the readers – the children and parents alike – for reading this book. I hope you can overcome your fears, too.

About the Author

"Music and writing, can't have one without the other..."

Annia Faith is a passionate writer and aspiring artist. She loves crafting stories and creating music that reach people on a deeper level. She hopes to make an impact in the lives of others.

Annia started writing at an early age, spending countless hours exploring the world of written imagination. As she grew, so did her passion for storytelling, leading her to pursue a career as an author. She hopes her future novels will touch the lives of many young readers.

Annia Faith continues to spread her love for both writing and music, inviting readers and listeners to join her on transformative adventures full of imagination and heart. Reach out to Annia via email at phazeproductions23@gmail.com. Also, check out her website at phazeproductions.store.

More reader acclaim for ...

THE BOY WHO FEARED THE WIND

❝The overall premise of the story is beautiful and simple, with a theme that all parents and kids can relate to in their own way. The illustrations are beautiful and so fitting to the story. I especially love how more color comes into the illustrations toward the end, when the boy begins to realize that taking risks adds more "color" to his life. Well done.

Kate Meadows
Author/Editor
Rapid City, SD

❝Facing fears is something that everyone has dealt with. Children are going to be able to relate to and have a connection with the boy in the story. It shows that this struggle takes time to get through but is possible. The use of color at the end shows life and victory over that fear. What a beautiful and poignant piece.

Jennifer Backhaus
Librarian/teacher
Rapid City, SD

❝Very well done! I thought it was cute, thoughtful, and was a good story about getting over your fears!

Emily Eisenschenk
Parent
Rapid City, SD

Made in the USA
Middletown, DE
16 November 2023

42855884R00022